ROMANS

Sin, Salvation, and the Love of God

Lifeway Press®
Brentwood, Tennessee

© 2023 Lifeway Press®
Reprinted Mar. 2024

No part of this work may be reproduced or transmitted in any form or by any means, electronic or mechanical, including photocopying and recording, or by any information storage or retrieval system, except as may be expressly permitted in writing by the publisher. Requests for permission should be addressed in writing to Lifeway Press®, 200 Powell Place, Suite 100, Brentwood, TN 37027

ISBN 978-1-0877-6731-4
Item 005838136
Dewey Decimal Classification Number: 242
Subject Heading: DEVOTIONAL LITERATURE / BIBLE STUDY AND TEACHING / GOD

Printed in the United States of America.

Student Ministry Publishing
Lifeway Resources
200 Powell Place, Suite 100
Brentwood, TN 37027

We believe that the Bible has God for its author; salvation for its end; truth, without any mixture of error, for its matter; and that all Scripture is totally true and trustworthy. To review Lifeway's doctrinal guideline, please visit www.lifeway.com/doctrinalguideline.

Unless otherwise noted, all Scripture quotations are taken from the Christian Standard Bible®, Copyright © 2017 by Holman Bible Publishers. Used by permission. Christian Standard Bible® and CSB® are federally registered trademarks of Holman Bible Publishers.

PUBLISHING TEAM

Director, Student Ministry
Ben Trueblood

Editorial Team Leader
Karen Daniel

Writer
Zachary Ethridge

Content Editor
Kyle Wiltshire

Production Editor
April-Lyn Caouette

Graphic Designer
Shiloh Stufflebeam

TABLE OF CONTENTS

04
intro

05
getting started

06
romans 1–4: our need/God's provision

34
romans 5–11: the result/reach of salvation

80
romans 12–16: the transformed life

108
God's good news is for everyone

INTRO

The apostle Paul was a devout Jew who opposed and openly persecuted the early church—that is, until he encountered Jesus on the road to Damascus. On that road, he experienced God's grace in a way that changed his life forever. His past was forgiven, and his future ambitions and plans were radically altered. From that point on, his mission was to share Jesus with Gentiles (non-Jews) everywhere he went. But he also desired for his own people to come to know Jesus, just as he had.

Paul's letter to the church in Rome is the most comprehensive explanation of the gospel in the Bible. His letter explores how all people are guilty of sin and are without excuse before God. The good news can only be fully appreciated when we understand the condition we all are in apart from Jesus.

If we are all sinners in need of a Savior, then how is it that we are saved? Paul made it clear in chapter after chapter that we are not saved by good works or by earning God's favor. Rather, we are saved by faith in Jesus alone. While we were still sinners, He died for us and made a way for us to have a restored relationship with God.

If God's grace is so available and free, should we just keep on sinning? Paul said absolutely not. God's grace doesn't just forgive our past; it also empowers a new future. As children of God, filled with His Spirit, we can have a transformed life. We can love our neighbor, overcome evil with good, and live in unity with other believers.

This lifestyle that God has called us to is not easy. We will face temptation, persecution, suffering, and hardship. But God reigns over all and can bring His good purposes from the worst of circumstances. As we trust Him with our future, let us be like Paul and share God's grace with the world.

GETTING STARTED

*This devotional contains thirty days of content, broken down into sections. Each day is divided into three elements—**discover, delight,** and **display**—to help you grow in your faith.*

discover

This section helps you examine the passage in light of who God is and determine what it says about your identity in relationship to Him. Included here is the daily Scripture reading and key verses, along with illustrations and commentary to guide you as you learn more about God's Word.

delight

In this section, you'll be challenged by questions and activities that help you see how God is alive and active in every detail of His Word and your life.

display

Here's where you take action. This section calls you to apply what you've learned through each day.

Each day also includes a prayer activity at the conclusion of the devotion.

Throughout the devotional, you'll also find extra items to help you connect with the topic personally, such as Scripture memory verses and interactive articles.

SECTION 1

ROMANS 1–4:

OUR NEED/ GOD'S PROVISION

We don't get what we deserve. It would be fair and right for God to withhold His mercy from us, but He doesn't. Our sin deserves punishment and death, but God wants to give all of us the gift of eternal life through Jesus. All it takes is faith in Him.

DAY 1

THE FOUNDATION

discover

READ ROMANS 1:1-18.

> **For I am not ashamed of the gospel, because it is the power of God for salvation to everyone who believes, first to the Jew, and also to the Greek.** — Romans 1:16

The book of Romans is a letter written from the apostle Paul to the church in Rome. Before Paul was an apostle, he was an enemy of the church, persecuting the early Christians. He was a devout Jew who belonged to a prominent group within Judaism known as the Pharisees.

But when the risen Jesus appeared to Paul on the road to Damascus, it completely changed the direction of his life. In that moment, Paul experienced the grace of God and was called by Jesus to share that grace with everyone all over the world. Paul received grace and authority to bring salvation to all people (see Rom. 1:5). He was made an apostle, someone personally called by Jesus to lead the church and declare His word.

Paul learned firsthand that God's grace couldn't be earned through good works. None of Paul's law-keeping could make up for his sin. His only hope was to look to Jesus in faith, trusting in Him for mercy and forgiveness. The good news of Jesus—that God's grace is freely available to all through faith—became the foundation of Paul's ministry. For that reason, it is also the theme of the letter to the Romans. In this letter, Paul will explain why salvation is by faith alone and how God's grace motivates the whole Christian life.

delight

In whom or in what are you putting your faith? Explain.

What are the main obstacles to your faith in Jesus? Do you struggle to believe that God will actually forgive you?

How can you help others put their faith in Jesus?

display

Just as Paul couldn't earn God's grace, neither can we. But we don't have to! It's available through faith. If you will trust Jesus, He will forgive you of everything you've ever done. Paul was the least likely person of his time to turn to Christ, but God saved him. You are not beyond God's grace and neither are the people around you. Who do you think is the most unlikely person in your life to follow to Jesus? Consider how God could use you to share the good news of the gospel with this person in the days ahead.

Lord, thank You for showing me grace that I could not earn. Help me believe that Your mercy is still just as powerful for me as it was for Paul. Give me Your heart for the world and show me how I can help others experience Your grace too. In Jesus's name, Amen.

DAY 2

FALSE FOUNDATION

discover

READ ROMANS 1:18-32.

They exchanged the truth of God for a lie, and worshiped and served what has been created instead of the Creator, who is praised forever. Amen. — Romans 1:25

God has revealed Himself through creation: His existence and power are displayed in the things He has made. Unfortunately, humans suppress the truth of God because we prefer to live our own way. We resist the reality of a Creator and allow some other thing to become our master, or worse, make ourselves gods. To some degree, every time we sin, we "exchange the truth of God for a lie" to worship and serve creation instead of its Creator (see Rom. 1:25).

As it turns out, things never end well when we fail to build our lifestyle on the truth. Believing the lie that God does not exist, or that we aren't really accountable to Him for how we live, or that His ways aren't best, leads to the profound brokenness we read about in this passage. As these verses reveal, a lifestyle that ignores God and His design for humanity ultimately degrades, enslaves, and corrupts us. Sin is never neutral. It always has a progressively worsening effect on our lives.

But the truth can set us free! When we receive God's truth instead of suppressing it, when we believe God's word rather than trading it for a lie, sin loses its grip on us. We are free to live in a way that worships and serves our Creator. When we live this way, we are free to be filled with His righteousness, love, mercy, and more.

delight

What truths from God's Word are you tempted to suppress or resist?

How does embracing God's truth lead to resistance from others?

How have you observed the truth of what Paul said in these verses through the way our world celebrates sin?

display

Carefully read through Romans 1:29-32 again. Take a moment to reflect upon the sins listed that you may struggle with the most. Try to identify things like why you struggle, the situations you are in when you fail, and how you might begin to make progress in overcoming them. We will not be perfect, but we ought to make every effort to grow in our obedience to the Lord. The sins listed here are common to all people; you are not alone in your struggle. But God does have something better for you. We can overcome sin when we believe and submit to God's truth.

Father, I need Your help to resist the lies of this world and live according to Your truth. Help me recognize the ways that I am resisting You or being deceived. Lead me in Your righteous paths so that I can worship and serve You as my Creator. In Jesus's name, Amen.

DAY 3

MERCY > FAIRNESS

discover

READ ROMANS 2:1-16.

> **Now we know that God's judgment on those who do such things is based on the truth.**
> **— Romans 2:2**

From a young age, children have a deep sense of fairness. They recognize when a sibling or friend gets an extra treat, doesn't play by the rules, or isn't held to the same standard. This sense of fairness is ingrained in the human conscience because our Creator judges according to the truth. As the apostle Paul puts it, "there is no favoritism with God" (Rom. 2:11). When God judges, He does so according to what is right.

God will repay each person based on how they have lived (see Rom. 2:6). No one will be able to say that God has judged them too harshly or unfairly. Paul even said that each person's conscience will confirm that person's guilt, meaning we will know in our hearts that God has been fair in His judgments (see Rom. 2:15).

But God's judgments aren't immediate when people sin. He is patient, restrained, and kind. God would rather be merciful than fair—He doesn't want to give us what we deserve. He would rather show us mercy. The kindness He shows us is meant to lead us to Him. Do not to delay or harden your heart. Instead, turn from sin and live for Jesus.

delight

How does Paul discourage us from being judgmental in this passage?

How can you imitate God by not showing favoritism?

What do you need to do in response to God's patience and kindness?

display

There are several ways we can apply the principles of this passage to our lives. First, Paul plainly says that we should not judge others, especially when we are guilty of doing the same things. Second, don't show favoritism, because God doesn't show favoritism. Third, support what is fair for all, because God is fair to all. And finally, be willing to show mercy even when people do not deserve it, because God has given you mercy you did not deserve. These are challenging instructions to follow, but if you live this way, God can and will use you to shine His light and influence others for Jesus.

Lord, thank You for being patient with me. I don't deserve the mercy You have given me, and I don't want to waste it. Please help me live in a way that shows others what You are like and points them to You. In Jesus's name, Amen.

DAY 4

INSIDE OUT

discover

READ ROMANS 2:17-29.

On the contrary, a person is a Jew who is one inwardly, and circumcision is of the heart—by the Spirit, not the letter. That person's praise is not from people but from God.
— Romans 2:29

The apostle Paul had some pretty strong words for those who took pride in their religious background but who were not living according to their beliefs. In these verses, he focused on people who knew the Scriptures, and who had even taught others, but whose actions undermined God's word. This kind of hypocrisy embarrasses God's name in the world (see Rom. 2:24).

In the old covenant, circumcision was an outward sign that someone was a follower of God. Though it may be a little confusing to follow Paul's point, here's the main thing: being a true believer is not about your outward religious activity or background. It's about God changing your heart.

Being raised in church cannot make you a true Christian by itself. Of course, it's a great blessing, just as Paul would surely have felt it was a blessing to be taught God's law and instructed in God's Word from childhood. But, as he was careful to point out in these verses, only the Holy Spirit can make someone a true Christian, by touching the heart and changing that person from the inside (see Rom. 2:29).

When the Holy Spirit changes your heart, the goal of your life is no longer to seek the praise of people but the praise of God. If our identity and confidence comes from our background, then we will seek validation from people. But when our confidence comes from the gospel, we seek the approval of God above all others.

delight

How can hypocrisy damage the reputation of Jesus?

Why is it important to understand that our background should not be the source of our assurance?

How can you live for the praise of God rather than the praise of people?

display

Having a Christian family background is a great blessing, but it should never be the source of our confidence before God. Our standing before God comes from what Jesus has done to redeem us and what the Holy Spirit has done to make us new on the inside.

Also, when we outwardly identify with Jesus, we must always remember that our actions affect His reputation. Think of the ways that you could bring Jesus's name more honor this week. Do the things that will show God's goodness to others, so that His name will be exalted among the people in your life.

Father, I want to bring glory to Your name through my life. Help me to overcome the ways that I may be hypocritical. Give me the confidence and peace not to live for the praise of people but to please You more than anyone else. In Jesus's name, Amen.

MEMORY VERSE

For all have sinned and fall short of the glory of God; they are justified freely by his grace through the redemption that is in Christ Jesus.

— Romans 3:23-24

DAY 5

EVERYONE NEEDS JESUS

discover

READ ROMANS 3:1-20.

What then? Are we any better off? Not at all! For we have already charged that both Jews and Greeks are all under sin, as it is written: There is no one righteous, not even one.
— Romans 3:9-10

The world is full of diversity: billions of people with very different cultures, ethnicities, and histories. Yet there are some things that are true of all of us, regardless of ethnicity or culture. One of those universal realities is that we are all sinners. In this passage, Paul quotes Psalm 14, reminding his readers that no one is righteous on their own. Someone's ethnic or religious background doesn't give that person a better standing before God, because every person has sinned (see Rom. 3:9).

Our rebellion against God is displayed in how we treat the creatures made in His image—that is, humans. Notice that the examples Paul gives of human sinfulness are dominated by the ways we misuse speech. We deceive, use sharp words, and curse. We harm one another verbally and sometimes even physically (see Rom. 3:15). This kind of sin against our fellow person is ultimately sin against God Himself. Rather than seek God, we turn away from Him.

This means that every person you know needs Jesus. There is not one person in your life who hasn't sinned or who doesn't need God's grace. We should begin by looking in the mirror and recognizing our own need for His mercy. Then, with humble and compassion hearts, we should look outward and see a world of people who need us to share Jesus with them.

delight

Why is there no advantage to being religious apart from Jesus? (See Rom. 3:9,20.)

Why is it so important that we recognize our own need for God's mercy?

display

Since every person needs Jesus, there is no place for pride or looking down on others. Our universal sinfulness ought to change the way we relate to one another. Be thoughtful in how you relate to people who are different than you. No matter the situation, work on changing your perspective to always remember your own need for God's grace. How can you be more humble toward siblings, friends, and even enemies? Change your thinking and let go of pride, and it will change your relationships for the better.

Father, I recognize my need for Your mercy because of my own sin. I know that I am no more worthy to be Your child than anyone else. Thank You for loving me despite my failures, and help me honor You today. In Jesus's name, Amen.

DAY 6

ALL FALL SHORT

discover

READ ROMANS 3:21-31.

For all have sinned and fall short of the glory of God; they are justified freely by his grace through the redemption that is in Christ Jesus. — Romans 3:23-24

Have you ever attempted something that you simply could not accomplish, no matter how hard you tried? Some people wish they could dunk a basketball, but can't jump high enough. Others may wish to be a singer, but don't have the vocal talent. There are some things that we will fall short of, despite our best efforts.

As the apostle Paul reminded the Romans, everyone falls short of God's standard. So, how can we be made right with God if everyone falls short? We are "justified freely by his grace through the redemption that is in Christ Jesus" (Rom. 3:24). God's acceptance is not something we earn; it is a gracious gift given to us through Jesus.

Since God doesn't accept us based on our performance, we have no reason to boast in ourselves. This would be like a young child bragging about his athleticism after someone lifted him up to dunk a basketball. He has nothing to brag about because the real work was done by someone else. It's the same with Jesus: He did the heavy lifting to bring us to God by dying on the cross. So, as Paul wrote in 1 Corinthians 1:31, "Let the one who boasts, boast in the Lord."

delight

How does God make us righteous through Jesus?

Why is salvation a gift and not something we earn?

How does God's grace remove our grounds for boasting?

display

Some people may be overconfident in their own moral standing and need to be reminded that they can't earn God's approval through their performance. But maybe you're on the opposite end of the spectrum. Perhaps you know how deeply you fall short and wonder if God will ever forgive you. You don't have to wonder anymore. Know that Jesus has done everything required to bring you back to God. Pray, seek the Lord, and follow Him, knowing you are forgiven and loved by God.

Father, thank You for forgiving me of all my sins. Help me believe that I am accepted and loved by You. Show me how to boast in You for all that You have done to save me, and show me how to not try to earn Your love or boast in myself. In Jesus's name, Amen.

DAY 7

THE BLESSING OF FORGIVENESS

discover

READ ROMANS 4:1-12.

Blessed are those whose lawless acts are forgiven and whose sins are covered. Blessed is the person the Lord will never charge with sin. — Romans 4:7-8

We aren't saved by following the law, but by God's grace through faith in Jesus. In today's verses, Paul looks back at Abraham, the father of the Jewish people. If Paul can show that Abraham was made righteous through faith and not works, he can prove that anyone can be made righteous in this same way.

God declared Abraham righteous before he was circumcised. For Abraham, circumcision wasn't the source of his righteousness but the sign of his faith in God, and that faith was the source of his righteousness. In the same way, our works are not the way that God forgives us but the evidence that we have been forgiven.

Paul's point was that God hasn't changed the rules. Just as Abraham was saved by faith, so all those who come after him will be saved in the same way. This was a great blessing to not just Abraham but to everyone. As David said, "Blessed are those whose lawless acts are forgiven and whose sins are covered" (see Rom. 4:7; Ps. 31:1).

This also means that salvation isn't something we earn. If our good works could earn forgiveness, then God would owe us forgiveness. His salvation would no longer be a gift. But God's salvation is a free gift, received by faith alone.

delight

Why would earning salvation through good works make it a payment instead of a gift?

How is Abraham's salvation by faith important for all people? (See Rom. 4:11.)

display

Everyone who has experienced God's forgiveness as a free gift is greatly blessed. Jesus has completely covered their sins. God will never charge them as guilty because His verdict is final. Their own thoughts may condemn them and Satan may accuse them, but Jesus has the final say.

So when those condemning thoughts rise, when you fail yet again, despite the fact that you have struggled so long, remember His verdict and receive His forgiveness. Nothing will set you free from shame like the power of God's free gift of grace. Live in the comfort and joy that comes from knowing your sins are forgiven by the great Judge Himself.

Father, You are the final Judge. Remind me of Your forgiveness when I am gripped with shame and regret. Help me walk in the power and joy of Your forgiveness. In Jesus's name, Amen.

DAY 8

AGAINST ALL ODDS

discover

READ ROMANS 4:13-25.

He did not waver in unbelief at God's promise but was strengthened in his faith and gave glory to God, because he was fully convinced that what God had promised, he was also able to do.
—Romans 4:20-21

God had promised Abraham that his descendants would become a great nation. The only problem was, Abraham was one hundred years old, and his wife Sarah was ninety. Yet they still didn't have a child. Nonetheless, Abraham continued to hope. Why? Because Abraham's faith was not in his own body or power. His hope was in the God who had created everything out of nothing. God had made a promise to Abraham, and Abraham was confident that God was able to do what He said He would do.

Abraham believed that God could—and would—do the impossible to fulfill His promise. But God's power to do the impossible for His people didn't end with Abraham. Just as God created life through two people who everyone else thought were as good as dead (see Heb. 11:12), so God brought Jesus—who *was* dead—back to life after three days. Death itself was no match for the life-giving power of God to fulfill His promise.

The story of Abraham's faith is an example to us. When we hope in the God who raised Jesus from the dead, we will experience God's power in our own lives. God did for Abraham what Abraham could not do for himself. We cannot raise ourselves from sin and death. But when we hope in Jesus, we will have life.

delight

Why can we hope in God even when our circumstances seem hopeless?

What does Abraham's story teach us about God's power?

How does Jesus's resurrection remind you to trust God, no matter what?

display

Abraham gave glory to God even before the miracle was performed. He believed the impossibility of his situation would only create a greater opportunity for God's power and faithfulness to be displayed, and his faith was strengthened through the experience. Consider the things God has used to strengthen your faith. How has God used even difficult things to grow your faith in Him? When life's challenges come at you, go deeper into your faith. Allow these challenges to be the platform upon which God grows your faith and receives glory through your life.

Father, when I face uncertain and difficult challenges, help me to trust Your power and faithfulness. I believe You raised Jesus from the dead and that there is nothing impossible for You. Please enable me to live in a way that demonstrates that faith today. In Jesus's name, Amen.

SECTION 2

ROMANS 5-11:

THE RESULT/ REACH OF SALVATION

When we were at our worst, God proved His love for us by sending Jesus. He did what we could never do on our own. He overcame sin and made us children of God. We no longer have to be slaves to sin. Our future hope is secure, and God will use us to share His good news with anyone who calls on Him for salvation.

DAY 9

OVERWHELMING EVIDENCE

discover

READ ROMANS 5:1-11.

But God proves his own love for us in that while we were still sinners, Christ died for us.
— Romans 5:8

When a prosecutor tries a case, she begins by collecting evidence. The goal is to prove who committed the crime based on the mountain of evidence so that there is no doubt in the jury's mind what the verdict should be. If we set out to prove God's love for us, what evidence would we gather to show beyond a reasonable doubt that God loves us?

Paul said the greatest evidence of God's love for you is this: while you were still a sinner, Christ died for you. The moment He decided to love you wasn't after you made improvements or turned away from sin. It was when you were at your most unlovable that God loved you in the most selfless way.

It's important to know that Jesus's death on the cross doesn't mean that God used to be mad at you and now He isn't anymore. No, God loved you before Jesus died for you. It was God's amazing and undeserved love that led Jesus to the cross in the first place.

It is for that very reason that we can say with confidence: God loves you. His love led Jesus to the cross, and the cross made a way for you to have peace with Him. Make peace with the One who loves you even when you are at your worst.

delight

How would you explain to other people that the cross proves God's love for them?

Why don't our hardships disprove God's love for us?

display

When we look for evidence of God's love for us, we often look in the wrong direction. We look to our circumstances, our status, our relationships, our family, or our health. While God's love may be seen in those things, they are not the proof of God's love. The danger of treating those as the proof of God's love is that we may then doubt His love when our circumstances change, or when our family goes through struggles, or when our health declines. God's love doesn't change with our situation. Today, look at that event that can never be undone: Jesus's death on the cross. There, God's love can be seen forever.

Father, thank You for the many ways You have shown me Your love. Help me to always remember that You loved me even while I was sinful and far from You. Empower me to live in the assurance of Your love. In Jesus's name, Amen.

DAY 10

A NEW REPRESENTATIVE

discover

READ ROMANS 5:12-21.

For just as through one man's disobedience the many were made sinners, so also through the one man's obedience the many will be made righteous.
— Romans 5:19

Every two years, citizens throughout the United States of America vote for the person they want as their representative. Those who are elected will go to the House of Representatives in Washington D.C. to represent the people who chose them. When you were born, you had a representative in D.C. who you did not choose but whose decisions had an impact on you nonetheless. When you grow up, you can help choose a new representative through the voting process.

A similar thing happens to us all spiritually. When we were born, we had a representative we did not choose. His name was Adam. Adam's choices had terrible consequences for us all. But we can have a different representative before God if we want. God sent Jesus to be a new representative for us—like a new Adam. Just as Adam's sinful choices brought death and judgment to us all, Jesus's righteous obedience can bring life and grace to us all.

We may object to the idea of having a representative like Adam. You may think, "It isn't fair that he represented us all." The truth is, we all would have made similarly bad decisions. Also, if we call Adam's representation unfair, by the same token, we'd also have to reject Jesus's standing in our place and receiving the punishment for all of our sins. Being represented by Jesus is greater than any way we could possibly represent ourselves before God. Our sin brings judgment, but Jesus gives grace that is greater than our sin to all who receive it.

delight

How do we know that all people have been affected by Adam's bad choices to sin?

What is possible now because of Jesus's obedience to God?

display

Although God's law reveals our sin, it can never reveal a sin that God's grace cannot cover. As Paul wrote, "Where sin multiplied, grace multiplied even more" (Rom. 5:20). There is no need to run from God or hide in shame. You can bring your sin to God with confidence that He will forgive you and cover your sin. He has an unending supply of grace. We only need to run to Him, knowing that because of Jesus, grace reigns supreme.

Father, thank You for sending Jesus to be my representative. I know I did not deserve it, and I am forever grateful for His obedience and righteousness. You deserve all praise and commitment, and I give that to You today. In Jesus's name, Amen.

DAY 11

FROM DEATH TO LIFE

discover

READ ROMANS 6:1-14.

So, you too consider yourselves dead to sin and alive to God in Christ Jesus. — Romans 6:11

When God gives us grace, it's not just about forgiving our past. It's also about giving us a new future. Grace means giving us something we do not deserve. We deserve judgment, but God gives us forgiveness. How does He do that? By transferring the penalty of our sin to His Son. Jesus took the death we deserve so that we can be forgiven.

Jesus was not the only one who died at the cross. The apostle Paul said that, in a spiritual sense, we died too. Our past, our failures, our sins were all buried with Jesus. But Jesus did not stay dead; He rose from the grave, and we were raised with Him. This means we get a new start. And that's where God's grace takes on another dimension in our lives. Not only does His grace give us forgiveness for the past; it also gives us freedom for the future.

We can walk in new life. We can live "dead to sin and alive to God" (Rom. 5:11). This is why we should not continue to sin for the sake of more grace. The grace God has already given us wasn't just to deal with our past but to redirect our future. Therefore, live in His grace every day as you die to sin and walk in obedience to Jesus.

delight

Why shouldn't we use God's grace as an excuse to sin?

What does it mean in your everyday life to consider yourself dead to sin?

How can you offer yourself to God every day?

display

Paul's application is clear: "Therefore do not let sin reign in your mortal body, so that you obey its desires" (Rom. 6:12). Look in the mirror and examine your life. How have you let sin rule over you? In what ways may sin be reigning in your life? Consider what it will take for you to be free of those sins. It may require great effort, sacrifice, and accountability. Begin to take steps today to make that freedom a reality. You can be free if you will listen to God's word and do what Paul says in these verses.

Father, I look to You for the grace to walk away from my sin and into the good works You have for me. Please give me the strength to die to sin and live for You. In Jesus's name, Amen.

DAY 12

FREE IN CHRIST

discover

READ ROMANS 6:15-23.

But now, since you have been set free from sin and have become enslaved to God, you have your fruit, which results in sanctification—and the outcome is eternal life!
— Romans 6:22

What is true freedom? Biblical freedom is not the ability to do whatever we want. Rather, it is the power to do what is right. In our natural state, we are slaves to sin, bound by evil desires that lead to sinful choices. But notice that we don't merely go from slavery to freedom; rather, Paul says we go from slavery to slavery: "And having been set free from sin, you became enslaved to righteousness . . . since you have been set free from sin and have become enslaved to God" (Rom. 6:18,22).

This means that real freedom isn't found in total unrestraint, where there are no rules and no boundaries. Instead, freedom is found when we are in glad obedience to God. Paul described this freedom as obeying from the heart (see Rom. 6:17). The freedom God made us for is the freedom from sin we experience when our will is one with God's will. When Jesus changes our hearts, He gives us the desire to do what we ought to do.

This obedience from the heart should increase over time as we walk with Jesus. That spiritual growth is called *sanctification*, a long word that means we are being set apart for Jesus. He continues to get more and more of our heart and life. And in the end, we spend eternity with Him, where we are free from sin forever.

delight

How is the freedom described in today's verses different from how our culture thinks about freedom?

What steps do you need to take to change your view of freedom?

How might doing the right thing, even when you don't want to, influence your heart over time?

display

The goal is to do what is right because you want to, not because you have to. We should not wait to obey God until we want to do the right thing. Just like with any discipline or new skill, it is harder at first. But like the person who has been working out for years, eventually we will enjoy what is right. That heart change is what God wants to see in us, but it will never happen if we wait to feel like it before we begin. Obey God and the desire will grow for a lifetime.

Father, I ask You to give me the strength to obey You even when I don't feel like it. As I do, please change my desires so that I delight to do Your will. Sanctify me to live for You. In Jesus's name, Amen.

DAY 13

POWERLESS TO DELIVER

discover

READ ROMANS 7:1-14.

Therefore, my brothers and sisters, you also were put to death in relation to the law through the body of Christ so that you may belong to another. You belong to him who was raised from the dead in order that we may bear fruit for God.
— Romans 7:4

Imagine you were going on a student ministry trip, and when you got on the bus they told you that you had to sit by someone in your grade. Now, you might have done that anyway, but suddenly, now that there is a rule about it, you're tempted to sit by someone else instead. When you get to the event, they tell you to be in bed by 10 pm and not to leave the dorm until breakfast time. You probably wouldn't have tried to sneak out or stay up late, but now you are considering it.

There's nothing wrong with these rules; they are perfectly good and right. But once they've been introduced, they evoke an interest in breaking them that maybe wasn't there before. In these verses, the apostle Paul explains how something that is good (that is, the law) can be seized by sin to produce something bad (rebellion). Paul says, "When the commandment came, sin sprang to life again and I died" (Rom. 7:9-10). It's like that old adage: "Rules are made to be broken." The presence of the boundary can create an temptation to cross the line.

For this reason, the law is great at revealing our sin, but it is powerless to deliver us from it. It can teach us that something is sinful, but it can't empower us to do what is right. Therefore, Jesus came and radically changed our relationship to the law. He fulfilled the law and gave us new life so that we could bear good fruit for God (see Rom. 7:4).

delight

How does sin take what is good and twist it to promote evil?

Why is the problem within us and not with the law?

What did Jesus do to change our relationship to the law?

display

Jesus fulfilled the obligations of the law and showed us what it looks like to live in obedience to God. We are released from the bondage that comes from trying to obey God from the outside in. Rather, the Holy Spirit gives us power to serve the Lord from the heart. How can you follow Jesus's example and bear good fruit for God? Think of three things you can do this week to honor God.

Father, I know I cannot obey You in my own power. I ask You to fill me with Your Spirit so I can live in a way that pleases You. I want to bear fruit and display Your goodness to others. Lead me in Your righteous paths. In Jesus's name, Amen.

DAY 14

THE STRUGGLE IS REAL

discover

READ ROMANS 7:14-25.

For I do not do the good that I want to do, but I practice the evil that I do not want to do.
— **Romans 7:19**

Imagine a game of tug of war, with two teams pulling in opposite directions as hard as they can. Their aims are fundamentally at odds with one another, creating a massive struggle. The end result is that each team digs in, pulls with all their might, tearing their hands and wrenching their muscles in order to gain victory. This is similar to the struggle in the human heart and what it feels like to combat the desire to sin that still lives inside us all.

We want to obey God and to do what is right, yet we also desire sin and to do what is wrong. The Spirit of God has renewed our hearts and awakened us to what is right, but our sinful flesh won't go down without a fight. We are caught in this middle ground: God has changed us, and we know what is right, but we are not yet changed like we will be in heaven, totally free from the desire for sin.

This battle cannot be won by ourselves. The apostle Paul cried out in frustration at his struggle and looked to Jesus for deliverance (see Rom. 7:24-25). We must do the same. In our fight against sin, we need to recognize our dependence on Christ for true and lasting freedom. No amount of pulling, straining, or fighting in our own power will give us victory in our tug of war against sin. Only Jesus can give us victory over the desires of our flesh.

delight

What does it feel like in you when you experience the opposing desires described in these verses?

Why do we still struggle with sinful desires even after we have placed our faith in Jesus and been made new?

What can you do to overcome the desires of sin and to faithfully walk in God's ways?

display

No one this side of heaven will fully overcome sin. We all struggle with conflicting desires and are torn between what is good and what is evil. But God has not left us to our own strength. He will give you the power to win the battle through Jesus. Think of the situations where you tend to torn between good and evil. Determine now the strategy you will use to overcome temptation by focusing your heart on Jesus and doing what God wants you to do.

Father, I know that I am weak apart from Your grace. Empower me to follow Your will even when I have conflicting desires. Protect me from temptation and lead me to lasting freedom that sustains. In Jesus's name, Amen.

MEMORY VERSE

But God proves his own love for us in that while we were still sinners, Christ died for us.

— Romans 5:8

DAY 15
NEW IDENTITY

discover

READ ROMANS 8:1-17.

For all those led by God's Spirit are God's sons. For you did not receive a spirit of slavery to fall back into fear. Instead, you received the Spirit of adoption, by whom we cry out, "'Abba', Father!"
— Romans 8:14-15

God has done what we could never do by sending Jesus to suffer the condemnation we deserved and giving us His Spirit to live in spiritual freedom. We are not condemned, because Jesus was condemned in our place. We are able to obey God's law because Jesus fulfilled it. In our flesh we could not please God, but with God's Spirit we can obey His commands. Our victory comes from Christ alone.

Because of all that He has done for us, we are truly free. We do not owe our sin one more week, day, or moment of our lives (see Rom. 8:12). Instead, we can leave behind our sin and live by God's Spirit. God has given us new identities—through Christ, we are children of God. So, when sin rears its ugly head and calls us to return to old ways and old habits, we can say, "That's not who I am anymore."

As a child of God, you are no longer defined by your worst mistakes or decisions. Instead, you are defined by what God says about you. And what He says is that "there is now no condemnation for those in Christ Jesus" (Rom. 8:1). Live in the identity that has been purchased for you by Jesus at such a high cost.

delight

How does your mindset affect your habits and decisions?

What sins do you need to forsake once and for all?

display

We cannot live in the victory that's possible through Jesus if our minds are in the wrong place. Our thinking will determine our living. Paul said, "For those who live according to the flesh have their minds set on the things of the flesh, but those who live according to the Spirit have their minds set on the things of the Spirit" (Rom. 8:5).

What can you do to set your mind on the things of the Spirit? What is causing your mind to drift toward the wrong things? Consider taking a break from social media, TV, or anything else that draws your mind away from living for Jesus.

Father, thank You for doing in Jesus what I could never have done on my own. Help me to change my mind set when it is leading me astray. Help me to put my sin to death by Your Spirit and live as Your child. In Jesus's name, Amen.

DAY 16

IT'S ONLY UP FROM HERE

discover

READ ROMANS 8:18-39.

For I consider that the sufferings of this present time are not worth comparing with the glory that is going to be revealed to us.
— Romans 8:18

For the believer, this life is as bad as it will ever get. In this life, we experience suffering, pain, distress, danger, persecution, and even death. But none of those things will have the final victory. The glory that is to come will far outweigh the sorrows we endured on our way there. The resurrection of our bodies will forever undo the power of sin.

But that day is not here yet. In the meantime, we wait patiently and with hope. We trust that the Holy Spirit Himself is praying for us even when we don't know how to pray for ourselves. We remind ourselves that God is still at work and He will not let our sorrows and struggles go to waste. Indeed, "We know that all things work together for the good of those who love God, who are called according to his purpose" (Rom. 8:28).

Our triumph is sure because Jesus is alive. We cannot be separated from His love, and He will secure our final victory. Therefore, we can trust God through any season. No matter the circumstances, rest in the love that was so great that God gave His Son for you (see Rom. 8:32). If He can bring good out of the cross, surely He can bring something good out of our trials as well.

delight

Why can Christians honestly say, "The best is yet to come"?

How can we have hope even when we go through suffering?

How has God's love comforted you in times of sorrow?

display

If you haven't yet, you will certainly face trials and sorrows in this life. It is an unavoidable reality. But even in our pain, God is at work. Consider how God has brought something good out of undesirable situations in your life. Think of how you can bring hope to others who are hurting in this season of their lives. Write them cards, or do something to show that you care. Through you, they can be reminded of God's love and experience it. When God brings good out of difficult situations, share that testimony with others.

Father, I look to You with hope. I trust that You have a plan, that You love me, and that You have a purpose for the things I am going through. Don't let me forget Your love. In Jesus's name, Amen.

DAY 17

UNEARNED AND UNDESERVED

discover

READ ROMANS 9:1-18.

So then, it does not depend on human will or effort but on God who shows mercy. — Romans 9:16

These verses, like several in Scripture, are difficult to understand. But they offer an important perspective on God's salvation—that God is the only One who can save, and He is free to show mercy in the way that He sees fit.

The apostle Paul grieved Israel's widespread rejection of the gospel. This is a theme that continues through chapter eleven. As Paul looked back at Israel's history, he explained that God's word never failed, even though not everyone who descended from Abraham followed God (see Rom. 9:6). God was and is righteous and faithful nonetheless.

Perhaps the most important point that Paul makes in this section is that God doesn't owe anyone His mercy and grace. In fact, grace and mercy are, by definition, treating people better than they deserve. If God owed us mercy, we would have somehow earned it, and in that case, it would no longer be mercy. As we saw earlier in the letter, if God's grace is earned, then salvation is not a gift but a payment for what God owes us (see Rom. 4:4).

The main point Paul wants us to learn here is that salvation is always a free gift of God. It's not something God owes us or that we deserve, but something that God gives by His own will and undeserved compassion. As the passage says, "So then, it does not depend on human will or effort but on God who shows mercy" (Rom. 9:16).

delight

Why is it important to understand that salvation is not earned and that God does not owe it to anyone?

How has God shown you mercy you did not deserve?

display

God's mercy is available to those who look to Jesus for salvation. This passage reminds us of the fate of men like Esau and Pharaoh, who rejected God's word and lived their own way. We should learn from their tragic mistakes and heed God's compassionate invitation. If you have not yet put your faith in Jesus, consider doing so today and talking to someone about what to do next. If you have put your faith in Jesus already, then what can you do to help others experience God's mercy?

Father, thank You for showing me mercy I don't deserve. When I consider the fact that You didn't have to save me—but did so lovingly, gladly, and freely—I am humbled by Your amazing grace. Help me live in Your mercy. In Jesus's name, Amen.

DAY 18

RECEIVED, NOT ACHIEVED

discover

READ ROMANS 9:19-31.

> **What should we say then? Gentiles, who did not pursue righteousness, have obtained righteousness — namely the righteousness that comes from faith.**
> —Romans 9:30

God's salvation doesn't operate on our terms. Humans try to obtain a goal by working and earning. Sometimes favoritism comes into play, as well. But, as Paul teaches us in Romans 9, God doesn't work like that.

God doesn't show favoritism to Israelites, but instead invites the distant and unloved to become His people also (see Rom. 9:26). Those who try to achieve righteousness by earning and working according to the law fail (see Rom. 9:31). God's righteousness is obtained through faith.

Even though this should make salvation easier, humans tend to reject this free offer out of pride. Salvation through faith in Jesus becomes a stumbling block to the human heart that is set on seeking to be "good enough" on its own. But God's way of saving isn't meant to display human achievement. Rather, God saves in ways that reveals His power and glory.

The one who earns salvation is the one who gets the glory, and Jesus is the only one who has earned salvation—not for Himself, but for all of us. He alone gets the glory and praise for the salvation we have received through faith in Him.

delight

How does God get more glory through salvation by faith?

Why do you think some people would rather earn or achieve salvation than receive it freely?

How do these verses remind us that God can save anyone, even those we think are least likely to come to faith Jesus?

display

You can never do enough good works, or go to church enough, or read your Bible enough to earn your way to God. God's salvation can only be received as a gift through faith. Who needs to hear this message in your life? How can you share this good news with other people this week? God will use you to bring others to Him, but you must look for opportunities and pray for boldness. Think of specific people with whom you can pray and share the good news of Christ as you have opportunities.

Father, thank You for saving people who are far from You. Thank You that no one is out of Your reach. Help me desire to bring others to You. Give me boldness and favor to be Your messenger. In Jesus's name, Amen.

DAY 19

SALVATION FOR EVERYONE

discover

READ ROMANS 10:1-13.

For everyone who calls on the name of the Lord will be saved. — Romans 10:13

The book of Romans teaches us several universal truths—that is, things that are true of everyone. For example, we are all sinners in need of God's grace. No one can save him or herself. In Romans 10:13, we discover something else that is true of everyone: "Everyone who calls on the name of the Lord will be saved."

While every person needs salvation, no one is beyond God's saving reach. What must we do to be saved? Paul said that we must believe that God raised Jesus from the dead and confess Him as Lord. When we believe in our hearts, God makes us right before Him. When we confess with our mouth, we receive a new destiny: salvation.

Being super religious cannot rescue us from sin (see Rom. 10:2). Someone could be a devout Jew, Muslim, or Hindu, but that wouldn't bring that person any nearer to salvation. Why? God's salvation isn't earned through our own goodness (see Rom. 10:3). That's like trying to score a goal in soccer by carrying the ball in our arms and running it across the goal line like in football. We could never score that way because the method itself is against the rules of the game. So it is with earning our own righteousness. Righteousness isn't earned; it is given through faith in Jesus.

delight

What happens when we believe in our heart that Jesus has been raised from the dead?

Why can't we be saved through religious passion and effort?

Who can be saved by Jesus? Defend your answer with some verses from today's reading.

display

Paul didn't just believe that everyone who calls upon Jesus can be saved. He had a genuine desire for people to experience God's redemption. He wrote, "My heart's desire and prayer to God concerning them is for their salvation" (see Rom. 10:1). So many of his Jewish countrymen were lost, not for lack of zeal but for lack of understanding and faith.

The same is probably true of people you know. They simply don't know the salvation that is available to them through faith. This week, pray every day that God would give you the same desire that Paul had: a longing for people to be saved by Jesus.

Father, just as Paul desired for others to be saved, give me Your heart for the lost. I ask that You would give people in my family, school, and community the courage to believe and follow You. In Jesus's name, Amen.

DAY 20

BREAKING NEWS!

discover

READ ROMANS 10:14-21.

So faith comes from what is heard, and what is heard comes through the message about Christ. — Romans 10:17

Imagine planning a party but never sending invitations. Would anyone come? How could they if no one told them about it? The same is true of the gospel. Jesus has died for our sins and risen from the dead. He invites anyone to come experience His forgiveness and mercy. It is the greatest invitation of all, but God sends it through us.

We are like mail carriers with the gospel, carrying God's invitation to the world. The gospel is available to anyone who looks to Jesus for salvation, but there's a catch. People cannot call out to Him if they don't know the good news.

In a parable, Jesus told His disciples to "go out into the highways and hedges and make them come in, so that my house may be filled" (Luke 14:23). The master in the parable had prepared a banquet and welcomed anyone who desired to come dine at his table. People may reject the invitation, as many did in that parable (see Luke 14:18-20), but the key is that his servants were faithful to invite people in.

The apostle Paul says that not all will believe the gospel (see Rom. 10:16). God held out His hands to people who defied Him (see Rom. 10:21). If people reject Jesus, that's on them. But if they never hear about Jesus, that's on us. We must share the good news with all people, so that God may reveal Himself even to those who are not seeking Him (see Rom. 10:20).

delight

How can you more intentionally be a bringer of good news to people in your life?

Does witnessing require us to speak? Why or why not? (See Rom. 10:17.)

What are some obstacles to sharing Jesus with others?

display

When you have good news in your life (such as a test result, an accomplishment, or a big win) you want to share it with the people in your life. Do you want to share the gospel with the people in your life? Paul's message to us is clear to see. We have a message to share, the greatest news of all. Remember that the gospel is good news, to be shared with joy. Think of three to five people you could share the gospel with in the coming weeks. Pray for them by name, and look for opportunities to tell them about the forgiveness that is available in Jesus.

Father, I ask for opportunities to share the good news with others in the coming weeks. Help me recognize those opportunities and have the boldness to share. Give me wisdom with each conversation, and soften other's hearts toward You. In Jesus's name, Amen.

DAY 21

NOT REJECTED

discover

READ ROMANS 11:1-16.

I ask, then, has God rejected his people? Absolutely not! For I too am an Israelite, a descendant of Abraham, from the tribe of Benjamin. — Romans 11:1

Earlier in the letter, Paul began to address the issue of Israel's widespread unbelief in the first century. If the majority of Jews in Paul's lifetime were lost, was that a sign that God had rejected Israel? Paul's answer is an emphatic, "No!" After all, Paul himself was a Jew. It's not that God had rejected them, but that Israel had rejected God and His prophets (see Rom. 11:3). Nonetheless, just as in Elijah's day, there was a remnant who were saved by God's grace.

God's desire is for the Jewish people to return to Him through Jesus. One of the things Paul believed would bring Israelites to Jesus was the inclusion of Gentiles into God's family. Sometimes when a new baby is added to a family, the previously youngest sibling gets jealous of all the attention the new baby is getting. Similarly, as Gentiles experienced God's saving grace, Jews would think, "Hey, I want that too!"

God wants all people to come to Him and experience His salvation. His grace is for the Jew and Gentile alike. Therefore, don't write any people off or assume that God is done with them. If they will put their faith in Jesus, He will receive them.

delight

How can we know that God has not rejected any people group?

How can seeing people come to faith in Jesus cause others to want to follow Him too?

What would it look like for you to want people to be saved as much as Paul wanted His fellow Jews to be saved?

display

The Jews knew the law, promises, and covenants, but they rejected Jesus. Nonetheless, God had not rejected them. You may know people who have dropped out of church or walked away from Jesus. They should have known better, but that doesn't mean you should write them off. Instead, you should long and pray for their return to the Lord. Who in your life has walked away from God? How can you help them come back to Jesus?

Father, I pray for those who have wandered away from You. I know You are not done with them, so help me to keep praying for their return. Use me as Your witness to bring people back to You. In Jesus's name, Amen.

DAY 22

THE G.O.A.T.

discover

READ ROMANS 11:17-36.

**For from him and through him and to him are all things.
To him be the glory forever. Amen. — Romans 11:36**

In sports, we often debate to who is the G.O.A.T, the "greatest of all time." Every sport has a shortlist of contenders, and loyal fans argue endlessly over who is truly the greatest. But when it comes to God, there can be no debate. He is in a category all by Himself.

Paul praised the depths of God's knowledge and wisdom and the brilliance of God's judgments and ways. When it comes to decision making, He doesn't need our advice. God needs no counselor. He has never been lacking or in need of help from anyone else. Rather, God is the source of all things. As such, God alone gets the glory forever.

Thinking back over what Paul has taught us through this letter already, we can see the unique wisdom and power of God. He demonstrates perfect love, forgives sins, never abandons us, and works in every situation for the good of His people. Surely, there is no one like Him, none more worthy of worship and adoration, devotion, and commitment.

Everything we have is from Him, so everything we do should be for Him. We could live for money, popularity, fame, or the praise of people. But those things will fade away; they are undeserving of our lives. Only God deserves our all.

delight

How can you see God's wisdom in the gospel?

How can your life show that God is great and worth living for?

display

As we see throughout the book of Romans, God doesn't owe us anything, for "who has ever given to God, that he should be repaid" (Rom. 11:35)? But the same cannot be said for us. When we consider all that Jesus has given us, we soon realize that we owe Him everything. When we give our all for Jesus, it displays His worth and glory to everyone around us. Think of how you can go further in your commitment to the Lord, so that all may say "God is awesome" and "Oh, the depth of the riches and the wisdom and the knowledge of God" (Rom. 11:33)!

Father, there is none like You. You are in a class all on Your own. I praise You for Your wisdom that is beyond my understanding. Help me show others a glimpse of Your greatness today. In Jesus's name, Amen.

SECTION 3

ROMANS 12-16:
THE TRANSFORMED LIFE

When we consider all that Jesus has done for us, it is clear that He deserves everything we have to give Him. If He has changed us, the world should be able to see the difference that He makes in our lives. God calls us to a life of selfless love, humility, and righteousness that is only possible through the power of His Holy Spirit.

DAY 23

THE TRANSFORMED LIFE

discover

READ ROMANS 12:1-8.

Therefore, brothers and sisters, in view of the mercies of God, I urge you to present your bodies as a living sacrifice, holy and pleasing to God; this is your true worship. Do not be conformed to this age, but be transformed by the renewing of your mind, so that you may discern what is the good, pleasing, and perfect will of God.
— Romans 12:1-2

Paul spent the first eleven chapters of the book of Romans teaching about the mercies of God. God's mercy demands a response, but what is the proper response? Paul said it's worship, not just with our words but with our whole lives.

Paul used the image of a sacrifice: it is as if we lay our lives on the altar for Jesus. It's about giving Him our whole selves, body and mind. Humanity does not naturally live that way, so being a living sacrifice will be an uphill climb. We will either be conformed to this age or transformed by God.

This transformation we need starts with God changing our thinking. If we think rightly, we can live rightly. Just as the mind tells the arms to move and legs to walk, so the mind tells the body to live for Jesus or for self. A renewed mind is able to discern what is good (see Rom. 12:2) and what is humble (see Rom. 12:3), and it looks for ways to use our gifts to serve the Lord (see Rom. 12:3-4).

This is what God's mercy is able to do. It doesn't just forgive our sins; it also changes our character and animates a life of worship to God. Be transformed this week, from the inside out, for the glory of God.

delight

Why is it important to understand that worship is more than just singing at church?

How is the world trying to squeeze you into a certain mold?

How can you be transformed by God?

display

It is far easier to be conformed to the culture than to be transformed by God. Why? Because sin is second nature to us. Also, every person is affected by the cultural assumptions that are common in their community. We subconsciously adopt worldly thinking through the media we take in and what the people around us consider to be good. Therefore, think about the ways that you are being conformed to the pattern of this world. What steps can you take to change your thinking to align with God's Word? Think about the ways God has gifted you and how you could use those gifts to serve in His church.

Father, I give You my body and mind as a living sacrifice. I want to worship You in how I think and live. Show me how You have uniquely gifted me to serve You and Your kingdom. In Jesus's name, Amen.

DAY 24

OVERCOME EVIL WITH GOOD

discover

READ ROMANS 12:9-21.

Do not be conquered by evil, but conquer evil with good.
— Romans 12:21

Whether in sports or in life, it's not just about winning; it's about winning the right way. Paul tells us to overcome evil, but there is one stipulation—we must overcome evil with good. We cannot defeat evil through evil means. It's possible to win the battle but lose the war because we ignored what was good and right for the sake of victory. In that case, evil would actually be defeating us rather than being overcome by us.

So, what does it look like for Christians to defeat evil? Overcoming evil looks like sincere love, clinging to what is good, and diligently serving the Lord (see Rom. 12:9-11). It looks like hoping and praying, blessing and not cursing (see Rom. 12:12-14). Overcoming evil looks like caring for those who are hurting and living with humility (see Rom. 12:15-16). Above all, it looks like rejecting revenge and trusting God's justice to make all things right in the end (see Rom. 12:17-19).

This kind of living is so contrary to the world's thinking that we could not imagine the impact it could have if we committed to such a lifestyle. The world would be blown away by the transforming power of the gospel if the church would live this way. But it starts with each person committing to these values. Don't wait for others to go first. You lead the way and show the world what it looks like for good to triumph over evil.

delight

How can acting out of genuine love and goodness affect our witness?

How can we resist the temptation to take revenge?

What does it look like for us to love our enemies?

display

Paul explained how to love our enemies, but it is much easier said than done. We would rather get revenge, even the score, or get the final word. But Paul told us to let God have the final word. Judgment belongs to Him. It is our job to love everyone and trust God.

When you read through Romans 12:9-21, which characteristics stand out to you? What areas do you need to work on the most? We all have room to grow, so choose at least two areas you will put intentional effort towards improving this week. Finally, commit that you are not going to seek revenge, no matter what.

Father, this world is full of so much evil, and I want to be a light and an example of goodness. Help me live these qualities even when I don't feel like it. Show me where I need to improve, and help me to trust You with the outcome. In Jesus's name, Amen.

DAY 25

LOVE YOUR NEIGHBOR

discover

READ ROMANS 13:1-14.

> **The commandments, Do not commit adultery; do not murder; do not steal; do not covet; and any other commandment, are summed up by this commandment: Love your neighbor as yourself.** — Romans 13:9

Life is full of obligations: authorities to obey, homework to complete, chores to do, practices to attend, and teammates to work with. But Paul says our greatest obligation is to love one another. What does it look like to love one another?

The second half of the Ten Commandments is a great place to start (see Rom. 13:9). The law gives us specific ways to love our neighbor by not sinning against them. True love "does no wrong to a neighbor" (Rom. 13:10). Loving our neighbor is of utmost importance and urgency. Paul said now is the time to wake up from our slumber and walk in the light.

One way we love our neighbor is by living righteously. Paul said to be sexually pure and to walk with decency. He also warned against jealously and fighting. How can we do these things? We must put on the Lord Jesus Christ. He is the perfect example of love. He shows us how to love our neighbor and live in godliness. Sometimes we think those things are positioned against one another, as if we must choose between love and godliness. But Paul wrote elsewhere that "love finds no joy in unrighteousness" (1 Cor. 13:6). Jesus never had to choose between sin or love, and neither do we. Jesus shows us how to do both perfectly, so follow His example today.

delight

What reason does Paul give for us to obey authorities?

What are some ways you struggle to love your neighbor?

What does it looks like to "put on the Lord Jesus Christ" as Paul said in Romans 13:14?

display

We have all failed to love one another like we ought to, but God has given us another opportunity to love others as He has loved us. His love is humble, selfless, and sacrificial. Love is not an abstract idea; it is expressed in simple, everyday actions. Love by telling the truth, by offering encouragement, by serving others, and more. Think of three ways you can show love this week, and don't go to sleep without doing at least one of them every single day.

Father, thank You for loving me perfectly. I need Your help to love my neighbor as myself. Open my eyes to the ways I can show love every day, starting today. In Jesus's name, Amen.

DAY 26

MOUNTAINS AND MOLEHILLS

discover

READ ROMANS 14:1-12.

Welcome anyone who is weak in faith, but don't argue about disputed matters. — Romans 14:1

Some things are simply black and white, but life is not always so simple. In the first century, some Christians believed you could not eat certain kinds of meat, while others felt it was permissible. Others believed that one day was most sacred, while others believed all days to be equal. Paul didn't say they all needed to agree. Rather, they needed to avoid quarreling and disputes.

Whatever one's conviction is over a certain matter, that person should be "convinced in his own mind" (Rom. 14:5), and he or she ought to do it for the Lord (see Rom. 14:6). It's not our job to change someone's mind; rather, our job is to make room for each other to not sin against their conscious.

The church, and culture at large, has too often lost the capacity to respectfully disagree. We draw lines in the sand, form tribes, and label those who disagree with us. This is not the way of Jesus. We ought to hold onto our conviction with a degree of humility, knowing that we will all stand before the Lord to give an account for our lives. Since God will be the Judge, we don't need to judge one another. Instead, examine your heart and be sure to live with a clear conscience before Him.

delight

How can we know if our convictions are right or misguided?

Why is it important to remember that we will all give an account of ourselves to God?

How can we learn to work with people we don't always agree with?

display

A sign of Christian maturity is the wisdom to know not that every hill is worth dying on. Yes, there are fundamental beliefs that cannot be compromised, but we shouldn't argue over every difference of opinion. In fact, unity should be the default and division should be the exception.

Have you elevated something beyond the level of its importance? Are you making a mountain out of a molehill in a relationship in your life? I encourage you to reevaluate and find common ground so you can work with Christians you don't always agree with.

Father, I ask You to give me wisdom and discernment to determine my convictions. I also ask You to show me areas where I should be willing to agree to disagree with others. I look to You for guidance and ask for a heart of unity towards other believers. In Jesus's name, Amen.

MEMORY VERSE

Therefore, brothers and sisters, in view of the mercies of God, I urge you to present your bodies as a living sacrifice, holy and pleasing to God; this is your true worship. Do not be conformed to this age, but be transformed by the renewing of your mind, so that you may discern what is the good, pleasing, and perfect will of God.

— Romans 12:1-2

DAY 27

LOVE OVER LIBERTY

discover

READ ROMANS 14:13-23.

So then, let us pursue what promotes peace and what builds up one another. — Romans 14:19

In math, there are rules about how to solve a problem that tell us the order to work through the equation. In English, there are rules about when and how to use certain words, such as "I" and "me." When making ethical decisions, we must also consider a variety of factors to decide whether we should do something or not.

One of those factors is to ask, "How will this affect other people and their faith?" Something may not be sinful itself, but it still might harm someone else's faith. When choosing between our Christian liberty and love for someone else, we should always choose love. As Paul wrote, "For if your brother or sister is hurt by what you eat, you are no longer walking according to love. Do not destroy, by what you eat, someone for whom Christ died" (Rom. 14:15).

When we put others ahead of our own freedom, we are serving Christ and building one another up. And when it is right to exercise our Christian liberty, it should always be done in faith. Righteous living is always by faith, with a clear conscience toward God. As Paul told us in the opening chapter, "The righteous will live by faith" (Rom. 1:17).

delight

Why is it important to understand that our actions can cause someone else to stumble?

How does prioritizing love put others before ourselves? How does prioritizing liberty puts ourselves first?

What can you do to promote peace in your family, school, and in your church?

display

Paul wanted the Roman Christians to focus on building one another up. That would be a worthwhile goal for all of us. Think of the people God has used to build you up. What did they do to encourage you and help you grow? Consider ways that you could do that for other people.

All of us want to be around people who lift us up and motivate our faith. You could be that kind of person this week, but it will take intentionality. Take a moment each morning to think of who you can build up that day and how you will do it.

Father, I see that so many people are tearing others down, but I know You want me to build people up. Please help me overcome my own self-centeredness and see the opportunities I have to promote peace. In Jesus's name, Amen.

DAY 28

STRENGTH FOR SELFLESS LIVING

discover

READ ROMANS 15:1-13.

Now may the God who gives endurance and encouragement grant you to live in harmony with one another, according to Christ Jesus. — Romans 15:5

A few years ago, I was in a workout group with some men who would gather to exercise and run. When we would run, those who finished first would always circle back to the guys in the back and run with them to the finish line. Despite their own exhaustion, they would selflessly consider those who were weaker and use their remaining energy to build them up and help then finish.

God calls us to the same mentality in the Christian race. We should run together as one united family. Along the journey, God gives us endurance and encouragement to press on and work in harmony with one another. Through it all, God gets glory when we serve one another and live in unity.

Jesus has shown us how to live in harmony with each other. He did not live for selfish gain; He endured insults but was humble in return. Though He was the promised King, the ruler over all, He used His authority to lift others up and serve them. If our King would do that for us, how can we live in selfishness and pride?

A selfless life is not a joyless life. Indeed, God fills us with joy and peace when we live like Jesus. In God's economy, pleasing yourself is a path toward misery but living to please others brings joy. Run the race and bring as many people along with you as you can.

delight

How can the stories of Scripture show us how to run with hope and endurance? (See Rom. 15:4.)

Why is it important to live in harmony with one another?

What can you do to encourage others who are weak and struggling?

display

The Christian life may sometimes be tiring. You may at times want to throw in the towel. But God will give you the strength you need for each day. Our endurance does not come from our own power, but from His encouragement. He will fill you with hope, and empower you to press on.

When you feel like giving up, where do you turn? When you are tired, what do you look to for strength? We may be tempted to turn to vices, but God says to look to Him. He will fill us with the strength and hope we need to keep living for Him.

Father, I look to You for the encouragement and power I need to live for You. Give me Your joy so that I can lift other believers up every day. In Jesus's name, Amen.

DAY 29

#GOALS

discover

READ ROMANS 15:14-33.

My aim is to preach the gospel where Christ has not been named, so that I will not build on someone else's foundation.
— Romans 15:20

What are your goals? You may have goals in school, goals for athletics, or relationship goals. But what about your spiritual goals? What do you want to accomplish for Jesus? The apostle Paul's goal was to preach Jesus where the gospel had not yet been proclaimed.

History is filled with pioneers, people who go where no one else has gone before. Think of people like Thomas Edison, Albert Einstein, Rosa Parks, and Amelia Earhart. Paul wanted to be a pioneer for Christ, taking the good news of Jesus where there were no Christians and no churches.

The church still needs people with this ambition. There are approximately three billion people who have not heard the gospel of Jesus.[1] The Great Commission—to make disciples of all people—should be the greatest priority of the church (see Matt. 28:19-20). Paul has shown us throughout Romans how every person is a sinner in need of God's mercy. As long as people have not heard the gospel, the church's mission remains unfinished.

God is still sending people to be pioneers for the gospel. Perhaps you could be someone who will take the gospel to people who need it most. We should be discontent with the fact that so many still don't have access to the gospel. Pray that God would give you His heart for the nations and use you to advance His mission to redeem the world.

[1] David Platt, "Great Commission Statistics that Should Concern Us," Radical, May 5, 2021, https://radical.net/article/great-commission-statistics-that-should-concern-us/.

delight

Why do we need to take the gospel to the whole world?

How can we increase our love for the nations?

Who still needs to hear the gospel in your life?

display

The Great Commission is the calling of all believers. We all have a role to play in God's mission. Sharing the gospel is not reserved for pastors, ministers, teachers, or missionaries.

As a follower of Jesus, what are your goals? What do you want to accomplish with your life? Our goals tend to be related to earthly advancement and achievement. But what if our greatest ambition was reserved for building God's kingdom? Think of how you can be used by God in this season of your life to share the gospel. Talk to a pastor about going on a mission trip. Learn more about unreached people groups, and begin to pray for their salvation and for the missionaries who are taking the gospel to the ends of the earth.

Father, thank You for the faithful Christians who came before me, shared the gospel, and passed the good news to me. Increase my heart for the nations and show me how I can be a part of your mission. In Jesus's name, Amen.

DAY 30
CAN'T DO IT ALONE

discover

READ ROMANS 16:1-27.

The God of peace will soon crush Satan under your feet. The grace of our Lord Jesus be with you.
— Romans 16:20

The closing chapter of Romans is dominated by a list of personal remarks and messages. It seems evident that Paul loved people on a personal level and built meaningful relationships with the people he served with. His words serve as a reminder that none of us can live the transformed life on our own. We need other believers building us up and partnering with us to accomplish God's mission.

The church is full of people with a variety of gifts and backgrounds, and each one has the potential to contribute to God's kingdom. Paul didn't try to live out his calling alone, and neither should you. It's not only important to have good people in your life; it is also important to avoid the wrong people. There will always be those who want to divide and create problems. Paul said to avoid them because such people are only serving their own agenda and not Jesus.

Though some people build up and other people try to tear down, one thing is sure: God will defeat Satan (see Rom. 16:20). God will strengthen His people to do His will, advance His gospel, and bring Him glory. He is the wise God who will direct human history and our lives to His good and perfect will.

delight

Who would you consider your partners in living for Jesus?

How can you help one another fulfill the purpose God has for your lives?

Why is it important to avoid relationships that drag you away from God's plan and purpose for you?

display

You cannot overestimate the influence that others can have on your success as a Christian. So many people contributed to Paul's life, and he took the time to show gratitude for their friendship and service. Take a moment to reflect on the people who have had a great impact on your life. Following Paul's example, write these people a note or call them to express your gratitude for their help and support. It will encourage them to keep living for Jesus and remind you of God's faithfulness in your life.

Finally, take a moment to evaluate the relationships that may be taking you away from God. How can you prevent others from pulling you away from the life God wants you to live? Determine in your heart that you will either be a positive influence or be willing to step away from a situation that is leading you down the wrong path.

Father, thank You for the amazing people You have placed in my life. I would not be where I am without their influence and support. In each season, lead me to relationships that will bring me closer to You and help me live for Your glory. In Jesus's name, Amen.

God's Good News for Everyone

According to author Timothy Keller, "[the book of] Romans is, at its heart, a letter about the gospel."[1] We hear this word, *gospel*, a lot. It summarizes the four books of the Bible (Matthew, Mark, Luke, and John) that give eyewitness accounts of Jesus's life, ministry, death, and resurrection. We hear it described as a message that tells about our need for a Savior—the Savior God provided—and what that means for us. And it also describes the focal point of that message: Jesus.

We, like Paul, are called to be messengers of this gospel, this incredibly good news. Over the last thirty days, you've examined our need and God's provision regarding sin, the result and reach of salvation, and how our lives are transformed when we say yes to the invitation Jesus extends: Come, follow Me.

Maybe you'll one day go to a foreign country to share the gospel on a mission trip or be a missionary who carries the gospel to people who have never heard the good news. But maybe that's not what God has called you to do. Regardless, you can always share the gospel with the people around you as you go through life. And that's something you can begin doing today.

---

[1] Timothy Keller, *Romans 1–7 for You*, ed. Carl Laferton (The Good Book Company, 2014), 11.

Complete the following to help you form an idea of who needs to hear and how you can share the gospel.

> **Draw a circle, then draw a smaller circle inside of that, and a smaller circle inside of that (three circles in total), each with enough room for you to write one name. In the outer circle, write the name of a person in your community who doesn't know Jesus. In the next circle, write the name of a classmate or friend who doesn't know Jesus. In the inner circle, write the name of someone in your family (such as a parent, guardian, or sibling) who doesn't know Jesus.**

On a scale of one to ten, how comfortable are you with sharing the gospel?

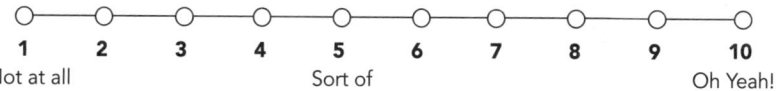

1	2	3	4	5	6	7	8	9	10
Not at all				Sort of					Oh Yeah!

Would that number change if the person who needed to hear was a family member or close friend? If so, how?

Part of being comfortable with sharing the gospel is having confidence that you understand it and know what to say. Sometimes, writing out the message before you share can be helpful. Choose one of the people from your circle, and in your own words, complete the following to write a guide for how you might share the gospel with that person.

Summarize our need regarding sin.

Summarize God's provision regarding sin.

Summarize the result of salvation.

Summarize the reach of salvation.

Summarize how our lives are transformed when we say yes to Jesus's invitation to follow Him.

Now, write a few sentences describing your own story of why and how you decided to say yes to Jesus's invitation (if applicable).

If you haven't said yes to Jesus's invitation, consider talking with your parents, small group leader, or youth pastor if you would like to do that.

Now, look back at the names in the other two circles. On a separate sheet of paper, complete the same process with those specific people in mind.

It's important to realize that God and His message of salvation in Jesus never change; but it's always good to ask yourself how different people might need to hear the good news. Should you write it out in a letter? Grab coffee and talk about it in person? (See 1 Cor. 9:19-23.)

When we trust Jesus as Savior, we are given new life. Learning to walk in that new life can be tough sometimes, especially when it comes to sharing the gospel. Thankfully, all of Scripture is God's story, and Romans helps us see ourselves and our need for Jesus in every chapter.

You know the story. You know the Storyteller. What will you do with the good news you've been given?

LIFEWAY STUDENT DEVOTIONS
Engage with God's Word.

lifeway.com/teendevotionals

- [ ] YOUR WILL BE DONE

- [ ] SPIRIT & TRUTH

- [ ] THREE-IN-ONE

- [ ] IN THE BEGINNING

- [ ] TRUTH AND LOVE

- [ ] SEARCH AND KNOW

- [ ] TAKE UP AND FOLLOW

- [ ] THE SHEPHERD KING

- [ ] CHARACTER & COURAGE

- [ ] WORDS OF WISDOM

- [ ] PIONEER & PERFECTOR

- [ ] WITH YOU